Goodnight,
Monster

Other titles in the First Young Puffin series

Goodnight, Monster

Written and illustrated by
Carolyn Dinan

PUFFIN BOOKS

For Daisy, Florence and Lizzie

PUFFIN BOOKS

Published by the Penguin Group
Penguin Books Ltd, 27 Wrights Lane, London W8 5TZ, England
Penguin Putnam Inc., 375 Hudson Street, New York, New York 10014, USA
Penguin Books Australia Ltd, Ringwood, Victoria, Australia
Penguin Books Canada Ltd, 10 Alcorn Avenue, Toronto, Ontario, Canada M4V 3B2
Penguin Books (NZ) Ltd, Private Bag 102902, NSMC, Auckland, New Zealand

Penguin Books Ltd, Registered Offices: Harmondsworth, Middlesex, England

First published by Hamish Hamilton Ltd 1992
Published in Puffin Books 1997
5 7 9 10 8 6

Copyright © Carolyn Dinan, 1992
All rights reserved

The moral right of the author and illustrator has been asserted

Printed in Hong Kong by Midas Printing Limited

It was late but Dan wasn't tired.

"Tell me a story, Mum, please," he begged. "Just a little one."

"It's too late for any more stories," said Mum. "Go to sleep."

"I can't sleep," said Dan. "I'm thirsty."

"There's a glass of water by your bed," said Mum.

"I'm too hot," Dan complained.

"I'll open the window," said Mum. "How's that?"

"I'm lonely," said Dan.

"You can't be lonely," said Mum. "I'll only be downstairs. Goodnight, Dan. Sleep tight."

And she went away.

Dan couldn't sleep. He stared out the window at the moon. Then he watched the shapes the shadows made on the floor and on the wall behind his bed. One shadow was bigger than all the others.

"Like a Monster," thought Dan. "But it's just my own shadow, really."

He wiggled his fingers but the shadow
stayed the same. Then he kept very still but
the shadow began to move. It swayed
slowly from side to side, getting bigger and
bigger . . .

"MUM!" called Dan. "Oh Mum! There's a Monster under my bed and it keeps jumping out – I can see its shadow!"

Mum ran in and pulled the curtains across the window.

"That's only the old apple tree in the garden," she said. "You don't need to worry about that. Now, close your eyes and go to sleep."

Dan closed his eyes tight. He rolled over and his quilt slipped to the floor. He pulled it back quickly.

"That felt like someone tugging my quilt off," thought Dan. "But of course it wasn't. I'll just check there's no one there."

Dan opened his eyes and saw two large
hairy feet sticking out from under his bed.

"Mum!" wailed Dan. "Hurry, Mum! There's a Monster under my bed! I can see its FEET!"

Mum ran into the room and looked under the bed.

"It's your new furry slippers, Dan," she smiled, picking them up. "Look! What a fuss about nothing. Now, go to sleep."

Dan still couldn't sleep. He listened to himself breathing. It sounded very loud. Then he held his breath. The breathing went on.

"I expect it's just me I hear, breathing through my nose," thought Dan. "But I'll have a quick look to make sure."

He hung over the side of the bed and peered underneath.

Big white teeth grinned back at him out of the darkness.

"Mum!" shouted Dan. "Come quick! There's a Monster under my bed! I can see its TEETH!"

Mum came upstairs and felt under Dan's bed.

"That's what you saw," she said. "It's just that terrible noisy toy Granny gave you. I thought we'd managed to lose that. What's it doing under your bed?"

Dan lay back and kept very still. He was
sure he could feel something moving under
his bed.

"Of course there's nothing there," said
Dan. "But I'll just make certain."

Dan leaned out of bed and stared bravely underneath.

Two round shiny eyes glittered at him in the dark.

"MUM!" yelled Dan. "Quick! There's a Monster under my bed! I can see its EYES!"

Mum came back slowly, knelt on the
floor and reached under the bed.

"Here's your Monster," she sighed. "One
roller-boot. I do wish you'd be more tidy,
Dan. Now, it's time you were asleep. I
don't want to hear another squeak out of
you until morning."

Dan listened to Mum's footsteps going downstairs. It was quiet in his room. The curtains moved softly in the night air, swish-wish, swish-wish.

Dan heard a small, sad sound coming from underneath his bed.

"Waaaahh," it went. "Waaahhh."

"MUM!" yelled Dan.

"GO TO SLEEP!" yelled Mum.

"But there's a MONSTER UNDER MY BED and it's going 'WAAAHHH!'"

"Well, tell it to GO TO SLEEP," shouted Mum. "It's much too late for a Monster to be awake."

Dan lay flat on the floor and looked right under the bed.

Two bright eyes looked nervously back at him.

"Oh," gulped Dan.

"Waah," whimpered the Monster softly.

"You should be asleep," said Dan severely. "It's very late."

"I can't sleep," said the Monster.
"There's a horrible Creature on top of my
bed. It's got hanging-down hair and big
round eyes and an upside-down face and a
great, big, open mouth. It keeps staring at
me and roaring. Ohhh, it's awful."

Dan thought about it.

"You must mean me," he said proudly.
"I'm Dan. You're quite safe with me. But
what a fuss we've been making."

"And then a nasty long arm comes swoop, swoop and takes away all my toys," wailed the Monster.

"That's my mum," said Dan. "You don't need to worry about her."

"Well, I do worry," said the Monster. "Anyway, I'm thirsty."

"There's a glass of water by the bed," said Dan.

"I'm too hot," complained the Monster.

"The window is open," said Dan.

"I'm lonely," said the Monster.

"You can't be lonely," said Dan. "I'm here."

The Monster sighed. It was almost a yawn but he turned it into a sigh.

"Tell me a story, Dan," he begged. "Just a little one."

"I can't," said Dan. "I'm too sleepy. I'll tell you one tomorrow night."

"All right," said the Monster. "Goodnight, Dan."

"Goodnight, Monster," said Dan.

And they went to sleep.

Also available in First Young Puffin

THE DAY THE SMELLS WENT WRONG
Catherine Sefton

It is just an ordinary day, but Jackie and Phil can't
understand why nothing smells as it should. Toast
smells like tar, fruit smells like fish, and their school
dinners smell of perfume! Together, Jackie and Phil
discover the cause of the problem . . .

DUMPLING
Dick King-Smith

Dumpling wishes she could be long and sausage-shaped
like other dachshunds. When a witch's cat grants her
wish Dumpling becomes the longest dog ever.

BELLA AT THE BALLET
Brian Ball

Bella has been looking forward to her first ballet lesson
for ages − but she's cross when Mum says Baby
Tommy is coming with them. Bella is sure Tommy will
spoil everything, but in the end it's hard to know who
enjoys the class more − Bella or Tommy!